E
PI

Pinkney, Jane
The mice of Nibbling
Village

DATE			
FE 18 '87	FE 10 '90	NOV 23 '93	
AP 10 '87	AG 21 '90	JAN 30 '94	
MY 4 '87	SE 14 '90	APR 8 '94	
JE 3 '87	OC 8 '90	MAY 30 '95	
JE 18 '87	NO 8 '90	JL 11 '97	
	NO 17 '90	JUL 14 '98	
AG 1 '87	MR 6 '91	AP 06 01	
OC 31 '87	AP 14 '92	NO 23 12	
SE 26 '88	JE 26 '92		
NO 9 '88	FE 11 '93		
JY 20 '89	JE 19 '93		
NO 6 '89			

© THE BAKER & TAYLOR CO.

Do *you* know Mouse Nibbling?
Within your own home,
Quiet as the rain-drops
And light as sea-foam,
Under the floorboards
On delicate toes,
Mice run through the village
That no one else knows.

Illustrations copyright © 1986 by Jane Pinkney
Text copyright © 1986 by Margaret Greaves
All rights reserved.
Published in the United States by E. P. Dutton,
2 Park Avenue, New York, N.Y. 10016
Originally published in Great Britain in 1986
by MARILYN MALIN BOOKS in association with ANDRE DEUTSCH LTD,
105 and 106 Great Russell Street, London WC1B 3LJ
Designer: Riki Levinson
Printed in Hong Kong by South China Printing Co.
First Edition   OBE   10 9 8 7 6 5 4 3 2 1

Library of Congress Cataloging-in-Publication Data
Pinkney, Jane.
    The mice of Nibbling Village.
    Summary: The inhabitants of a mouse village go
about their daily lives, baking bread, reading by
candlelight, and cleaning house.
    [1. Mice—Fiction. 2. Stories in rhyme] I. Greaves,
Margaret. II. Title.
PZ8.3.P558683Mi 1986 [E] 86-11464
ISBN 0-525-44277-4

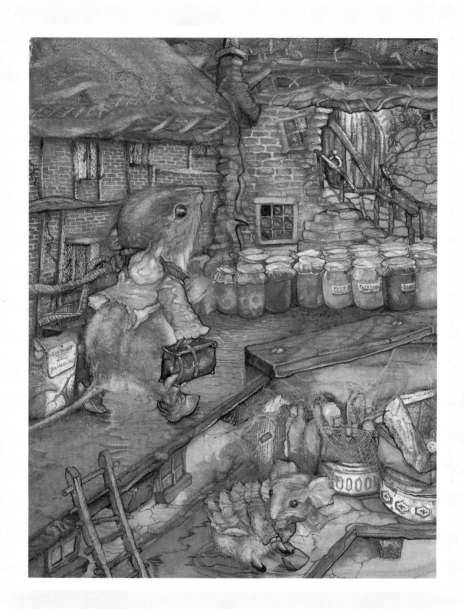

The Mice of Nibbling Village

pictures by Jane Pinkney

verses by Margaret Greaves

E. P. DUTTON · NEW YORK

Morrikin

Young Morrikin, it's very clear,
Will one day be an engineer.
He took the clock apart to see
Where, in the works, the tick might be.
But sadly, when he put things back,
The naughty mouse had lost the knack.
At seven that night the clock stopped dead.
"I'll make another one instead,"
Said Morrikin. He found a bell
From some old bike, and chains as well,
And wheels and string and pots of glue,
An ancient starting-handle too.
He's working still, but I don't know
If Morrikin's clock will ever go.

Busy Lizzie

With brush and duster, pail and mop,
This mouse is always busy.
She says her work can never stop.
They call her Busy Lizzie.

A speck of dust is a disgrace,
And dirty marks forbidden;
No spider's web can find a place,
However neatly hidden.

She mops the hall and sweeps the stairs,
The kitchen and the larder.
She dusts the tables and the chairs—
No mouse-wife could work harder.

When she has polished all the floors
You might think she reposes.
But no! She hurries out of doors
To dust the garden roses!

Miss Seraphina Sprout

Lady mice are lazy mice.
   They send their washing out
To the laundress of Mice Nibbling,
   Miss Seraphina Sprout.

She has a stone-floored kitchen
    as your great-great-grandma did.
She has jugs of boiling water
    and a wash-tub with a lid,
A board to scrub the sheets on
    and a heavy mangle too
For squeezing out the water.
    There's a dreadful lot to do
Before she hangs the washing
    on the pulley to get dry,
And settles to her supper
    with a rather weary sigh.
I think that Seraphina
    has to work too hard, don't you?
I'm glad that *I* don't wash the way
    Great-Granny used to do.

Mandy Snippet

In Mouse Nibbling it's always said:
"There's nothing so good as home-made bread."
Bread that tastes of the wind and sun
And the ripened wheat when the harvest's done,
Nutty and warm and sweet to taste—
Never a crumb of it goes to waste.
And of all who bake it there's none so good
As Miss Mandy Snippet of Mousehole Wood.
The loaf beside her is warm and fresh,
Just put to cool on its wire mesh,
And she's off to the oven again to see
If another one's ready—for you and me!

Mrs. Pepperset Brown

In a little old cottage in Tattlemouse Lane
Lives old Mrs. Pepperset Brown.
Whatever the weather, come sunshine, come rain,
She markets her eggs in the town.

She lives all alone but is happy all day,
For she always has something to do.
With her ducks and her hens
    and her guinea-fowl grey,
She has company all the day through.

Mrs. Trillaby Lee

Mrs. Trillaby Lee
Made cakes for tea
And topped them with strawberries
    and cream.
You never could eat
A more delicate treat,
Delicious and light as a dream.

They were lighter than air,
So you had to take care
To eat only what is polite—
Or you might float away
For a night and a day.
Oh dear, what a terrible plight!

Timothy Squeak

Now, Timothy Squeak
Came to stay for a week
With his aunt, Mrs. Trillaby Lee.
So she asked him to put
The cream and the fruit
On the cakes she had just made for tea.

But the cakes looked so nice
That Tim in a trice
Had gobbled up all on the plate.
Oh reader, take heed
Of Timothy's greed!
A sad ending I have to relate.

It's a year since that day
When he floated away
Like a wandering red balloon.
He's still drifting high
As the stars in the sky,
And he'll probably get to the moon!

Mattie

Something lives in Twitchett Lane
That no one ever sees.
But Mattie swears the thing is there,
And everyone agrees.

It bumps the windows in the night
And creaks upon the stair,
But when she goes to look for it
She finds there's no one there.

It puffs the washing on the line
And whistles down the lane.
But when she turns her head to look,
There's no one there again.

Its shadow flickers on the wall
Beside the village pump—
I think the wind is playing tricks
To make poor Mattie jump.

Mrs. Poppitt

Mrs. Poppitt loves to eat
From morn to eventide.
She says she isn't greedy,
She just has a hole inside.

At first she thinks her breakfast
Is the best meal of the day,
But then there's lunch and supper,
And a few snacks by the way.

And when at last it's bedtime,
When moon and stars are bright,
She has a little something
To help her through the night.

For any hungry moment
She keeps biscuits on the shelf.
I think that Mrs. Poppitt's hole
Is bigger than herself!

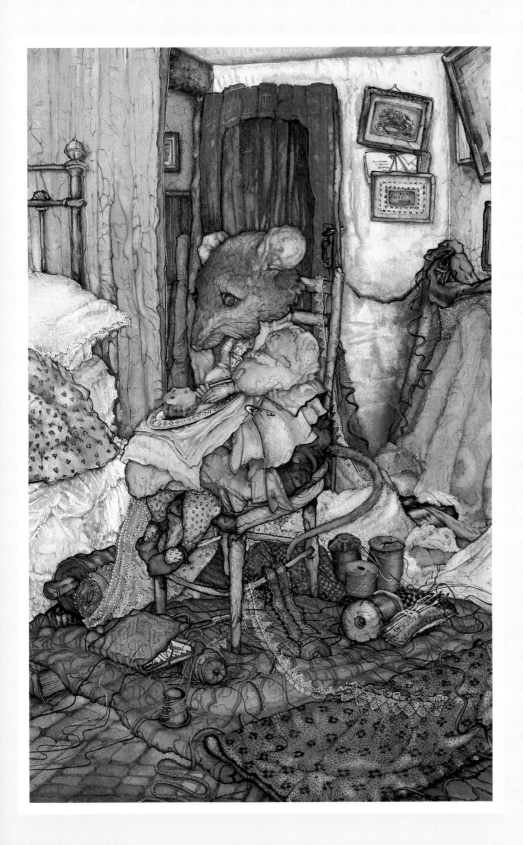

Aunt Taffy

Aunt Taffy is a nervous mouse.
She always double-locks the house,
And bolts the windows every night,
And draws the curtains very tight.

"Is that a ghost upon the stair?"
She listens to the listening air,
But nothing moves. The fire burns bright,
The saucepans wink with friendly light.
All's safe and still—until a squeak
Of hinges makes Aunt Taffy shriek.

The wind sighs in, the door swings wide,
Showing the starlit night outside.
Out of the dark a mouse comes through.
"Oh, Cousin Jane, I'm glad it's you!"

Dimity Moppet

Dimity Moppet wanted a gown
To wear at the Mouse Nibbling Ball.
She put on her bonnet and went to town,
But found nothing to please her at all.

Then Dimity looked in the attic and saw
Her granny's old sewing machine
And a white muslin dress that her granny once wore,
As pretty as any she'd seen.

"It just needs some colour," Miss Dimity said,
"To brighten the hem and the seams.
Here's fine scarlet silk and gossamer thread
That the spiders have left on the beams."

She twisted a pattern of silver and rose
That gleamed in the candle-light,
And everyone said, "What a beautiful dress!"
When she went to the ball that night.

Thimblekin

Here is little Thimblekin
Who ought to be in bed,
But feeling very wide-awake,
He's crept downstairs instead.

The kitchen makes him hungry!
He can catch a whiff of cheese
Mixed with the smell of new-baked bread
And celery and peas.

When she wants her peas tomorrow
His mother will find none,
For naughty little Thimblekin
Has eaten every one!

Belinda Bookery

When other mice are sound asleep,
Belinda leaves her home to creep
Into the human house above.
A clever mouse! She learned to love
Reading when she was very small.
That cat had chased her down the hall,
Where she had fled behind a shelf
Of story-books. She found herself
Stuck tight, with nothing else to do
But eat the dictionary through!
So, stuffed with words, she found that she
Could read the stories easily.
Now, by the guttering candle's light,
Belinda Bookery reads all night.

Thomas Ticklebrain

One night Thomas Ticklebrain tried to sing
The baby to sleep, but it cried.
So to soothe it he cleverly made a swing
In the light-bowl rocked by a piece of string,
And he tucked the babe inside.

"Hush, little mouse, in your warm cocoon,
Daddy has made you a bed,"
He crooned soft and low to a lullaby tune.
"Tomorrow he'll buy you a yellow balloon
And cherries and strawberries red.

"Hushabye, mousekin, swinging so high,
Daddy will rock you to sleep.
Tomorrow he'll go to the town to buy
Rafferty tart and cheesy pie.
Hush, little mousekin, sleep."

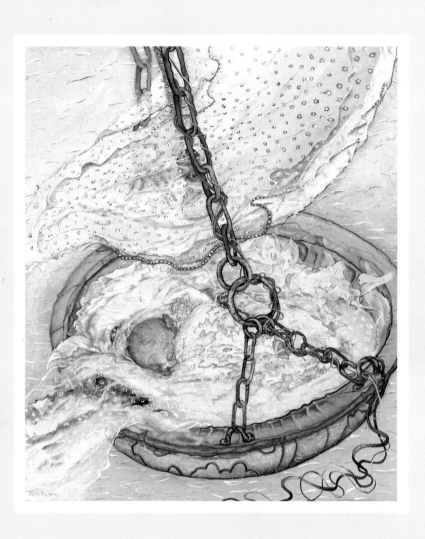